RHYME SCHEMER

RHYME SCHEMER

K.A. HOLT

chronicle books · san francisco

Library of Congress Cataloging-in-Publication Data

Holt, K. A., author.

Rhyme schemer / by K.A. Holt.

pages cm

Summary: A novel in verse about Kevin's journey from bully to being bullied, as he learns about friendship, family, and his talent for poetry.

ISBN 978-1-4521-2700-2 (alk. paper)

1. Poetry—Juvenile fiction. 2. Bullying—Juvenile fiction. 3. Friendship—Juvenile fiction. 4. Families—Juvenile fiction. [1. Novels in verse. 2. Poetry—Fiction. 3. Bullying—Fiction. 4. Friendship—Fiction. 5. Family life—Fiction. 6. Humorous stories.] I. Title.

PZ7.5.H65Rh 2014

[Fic]—dc23

2013032175

Manufactured in China.

MIX
Paper from
responsible sources
FSC
www.fsc.org
FSC® C101537

Design by Jennifer Tolo Pierce.

Typeset in Susan Classic and Flyerfonts.

10 9 8 7 6 5 4 3 2 1

Chronicle Books LLC

680 Second Street

San Francisco, CA 94107

Chronicle Books—we see things differently. Become part of our community at www.chroniclekids.com.

To my parents, Don and Carole Holt,
who made sure I grew up with a pen in one hand
and a book in the other

DAY 1

First day of school.
My favorite.
Easy prey.

Giant John.
A parade float of himself.

Freckle-Face Kelly,
like a painting
by that one guy
who drank too much beer
and went crazy.

Robin is so short.
I am a dinosaur
stepping on his lunch.
Plus,
his name is Robin.

So many
weenies.
So little
time.

• • • • •

King of the seventh grade
can't choose his own throne.
Assigned seats.
Not everyone's favorite.
Not *my* favorite.
But you know what?
My seat is next to
Freckle-Face Kelly.
Connect the dots,
all
day
long.

DAY 2

My brother Petey is in a band
so he always plays air guitar
while he lurches us over curbs
and through red lights
when he drives me to school.

His band is called
The Band with No Name
because it has no name.
Duh.

He and his bandmates can only think of
lame ideas for names.
Like the Flaming Turtles
or Midnight Pukefest
or Mustache Farm.

My ideas are great
but he never listens to me
only to music
with too many guitars.

I could learn the guitar.

• • • • •

Mrs. Smithson.
My teacher.
She has this mole.
I've named it Harry.
Not because it IS hairy
but because it's not.

That's called
irony.
I think.

Harry gives a shake
when Mrs. Smithson
sneezes
turns her head
walks too fast
laughs
hollers.

If Harry changes color
I would suggest
Mrs. Smithson seeks
a doctor
more makeup
a bag over her head
a Band-Aid
a black pointy hat.

DAY 3

Sometimes I wonder
about the coffee cups.

Every teacher has one,
even the PE teacher
who has so much energy
he seems to float just above the gym mats.

What's in those cups?
Witches' brew?
Ugly potion?
Bad hair broth?

It smells like coffee,
but judging from their breath
I'm sure it's way worse than just that.

I found the page in an old book.
No one will miss it.
No one reads those old books anyway.
The words just jumped out at me
like tickly little fleas
needing a good scratching.
So I scratched them.
And no one will know it was me.

. . . . .

I stuck it on the wall by the lockers
when no one was looking.
I couldn't help it.
I thought people would laugh.
People did laugh.
A lot.
Until Mrs. Smithson yanked it down.
She was not laughing.

We will die.
The smell is Killing us!
TEACHER SMELL is deadly.
Barf. ⟹

"We must hurry and get back to the road of yellow brick before dark," he said; and the Scarecrow agreed with him. So they kept walking until Dorothy could stand no longer. Her eyes closed in spite of herself and she forgot where she was and fell among the poppies, fast asleep.

"What shall we do?" asked the Tin Woodman.

"If we leave her here she will die," said the Lion. "The smell of the flowers is killing us all. I myself can scarcely keep my eyes open, and the dog is asleep already."

It was true; Toto had fallen down beside his little mistress. But the Scarecrow and the Tin Woodman, not being made of flesh, were not troubled by the scent of the flowers.

"Run fast," said the Scarecrow to the Lion, "and get out of this deadly flower bed as soon as you can. We will bring the little girl with us, but if you should fall asleep you are too big to be carried."

So the Lion aroused himself and bounded forward as fast as he could go. In a moment he was out of sight.

"Let us make a chair with our hands and carry her," said the Scarecrow. So they picked up Toto and put the dog in Dorothy's lap, and then they made a chair with their hands for the seat and their arms for the arms and carried the sleeping girl between them through the flowers.

On and on they walked, and it seemed that the great carpet of deadly flowers that surrounded them would never end. They followed the bend of the river, and at last came upon their friend the Lion, lying fast asleep among the poppies. The flowers had been too strong for the huge beast and he had given up at last, and fallen only a short distance from the end of the poppy bed, where the sweet grass spread in beautiful green fields before them.

"We can do nothing for him," said the Tin Woodman, sadly; "for he is much too heavy to lift. We must leave him here to sleep on forever, and perhaps he will dream that he has found courage at last."

"I'm sorry," said the Scarecrow. "The Lion was a very good comrade for one so cowardly. But let us go on."

They carried the sleeping girl to a pretty spot beside the river, far enough from the poppy field to prevent her breathing any more of the poison of the flowers, and here they laid her gently on the soft grass and waited for the fresh breeze to waken her.

The Wizard of Oz

DAY 4

If I was
short
wide
freckle-faced
I would beg for home school
or a ticket
on a boat
to Siberia.

• • • • •

Watch out, Sideshow Robin.
I'd take the long way to recess
if I were you.
I only suggest this
as a friend
because Giant John looks
grumpy
tired
hungry.
He might mistake you
for lunch.

• • • • •

Wait.
Can you take a boat
to Siberia?

DAY 5

The tires squeal
like Petey's car is making the road
screeeeeeam
in pain.

Get out.

I pull my backpack onto my shoulder
put my hand out
a fist bump
to say good-bye.

He just leaves it hanging.
A lonely bumpless midair fist.

I said, get out.

So I do.

The road screams again.
Petey and his air guitar are gone.

My fist hangs at my side now.
Heavy as a stone.

• • • • •

If I am stone
my fist is a gargoyle, scaring people away.

If I am stone
I don't have to answer questions in class.

If I am stone
I don't have to listen to all the boring things.

If I am stone
I am unbreakable.

If I am stone
My foot is jagged, cold, strong.

If I am stone
I don't laugh when Robin trips on my jagged foot
and slides down the aisle between desks
like he's a pebble rolling downhill.

I'm not always stone.

• • • • •

Mrs. Smithson.
That old meanie
with Harry the mole
jiggling in my face.

She made me go see
Hartwick.
Dun
Dun
Dun
Duuuun

He called my mom
but she didn't answer
so he gave me a warning.

BE NICE
OR ELSE

What a jerkface.

• • • • •

As a side note,
I have composed an ode
to Hartwick's tie:

[Clearing throat noise here]

O, Principal's tie
You make me want to cry
Because you are the color of
An armadillo butt

• • • • •

Another old book.
Another old page.
Just a quick sneak into the library.
Riiiiiiip.
The trick is to do it fast
when someone is sharpening a pencil.
Noise camouflage.
(A good name for a band.)

• • • • •

A secret message
left from a secret word scratcher.
The teachers are not happy,
and that makes it even more fun.

A face with whiskers.
A grave face. A rat!
A rat likes to TALK.
Shove off I say. Stupid rat!
(h-a-r-t-w-i-c-k)

A brown little face, with whiskers.

A grave round face, with the same twinkle in its eye that had first attracted his notice.

Small neat ears and thick silky hair.

It was the Water Rat!

Then the two animals stood and regarded each other cautiously.

"Hullo, Mole!" said the Water Rat.

"Hullo, Rat!" said the Mole.

"Would you like to come over?" enquired the Rat presently.

"Oh, it's all very well to TALK," said the Mole, rather pettishly, he being new to a river and riverside life and its ways.

The Rat said nothing, but stooped and unfastened a rope and hauled on it; then lightly stepped into a little boat which the Mole had not observed. It was painted blue outside and white within, and was just the size for two animals; and the Mole's whole heart went out to it at once, even though he did not yet fully understand its uses.

The Rat sculled smartly across and made fast. Then he held up his forepaw as the Mole stepped gingerly down. "Lean on that!" he said. "Now then, step lively!" and the Mole to his surprise and rapture found himself actually seated in the stern of a real boat.

"This has been a wonderful day!" said he, as the Rat shoved off and took to the sculls again. "Do you know, I've never been in a boat before in all my life."

"What?" cried the Rat, open-mouthed: "Never been in a—you never—well I—what have you been doing, then?"

"Is it so nice as all that?" asked the Mole shyly, though he was quite prepared to believe it as he leant back in his seat and surveyed the cushions, the oars, the rowlocks, and all the fascinating fittings, and felt the boat sway lightly under him.

"Nice? It's the ONLY thing," said the Water Rat solemnly as he leant forward for his stroke. "Believe me, my young friend, there is nothing—absolute nothing—half so much worth doing as simply messing about in boats. Simply messing," he went on dreamily: "messing—about—in—boats; messing—"

"Look ahead, Rat!" cried the Mole suddenly.

THE WIND IN THE WILLOWS

WEEKEND

When I'm old
enough
I'll leave
this place.

Will Mom cry?
Will Dad miss me?

I can see them now
laughing together
about one less mouth to feed.

Will they worry?
Will they care?

Mom can use my room
for emails and bookshelves.
She will like that.

• • • • •

We are not rich,
though people think we are.
I'm sick of it.

Get it?
Sick?
'Cause Mom and Dad are doctors.

If we were rich I'd have a dirt bike
instead of four brothers.

Patrick, Paul, Philip, Petey.
One two three four barf.
At least I have my own room.

DAY 6

Numbering the school days
in this notebook
might be
a
Very
Bad
Idea.

It's making the school year
long
longer
longest.

And the second week
just started.

• • • • •

I don't know a lot about tornadoes,
but I saw one last year.
Longest five minutes of my life.
Even longer than the
first week of school
which was just
really
freaking
long.

That tornado looked like
someone was putting our
street into a
blender.

Chunks of road mixed with cars.
Trees mixed with windows.
The noise was
so loud.

It was so loud it was almost quiet.
Like how every color mixed together
makes the color
white.

No one was home except for me and Petey.
His face, the same green as the sky,
his feet stuck to the carpet
like the trees used to
stick in the
ground.

Come on! Come on! Come on! I shouted
and he wouldn't move.
He wouldn't move.
We were easy prey.
So I grabbed him
by the shirt
and pulled
and pulled
and pulled.

Then he was with me in the Harry Potter closet
under the stairs
my arms over
his head.

And the blender roared by
and Petey cried hard
with my arms still there
still over
his head.

And then the big, messy racket was gone.
Petey sniffed real big and said
What are you staring at?
YOU'RE the baby
in this
family.

And he's hated me.
Hated me
ever
since.

•　•　•　•　•

I feel like that tornado,
that blender in the sky,
jumped down my throat
and is now buried inside.

• • • • •

The blob of sauce
drips off his ear
in
slow motion.

His empty bowl
sits on his head
a
crooked hat.

My hand on my mouth
not really covering
the
snorts of laughter.

Spaghetti and meatballs
the same color
as
Robin's hair.

Robin
doesn't think
it's so funny.

Neither does
Harry
the mole.

Now I wait for
Hartwick.

Again.

• • • • •

If I stare at the stain on the ceiling
I don't have to stare at Hartwick
while he says
Woh woh woh
and tells me to
STRAIGHTEN UP.

He called my mom
but she didn't answer.
Again.
So he gave me
another warning.

But
THE NEXT TIME
he says
while I stare at the stain
THERE WILL BE MAJOR CONSEQUENCES
. . .
MISTER

He is still
a jerkface.

• • • • •

As a side note,
I have composed another ode
to Hartwick's tie:

[Clearing throat noise here]

O, Principal's tie
You make me want to puke
Because you are the color of
Squishy, moldy fruit

• • • • •

There is this word:
Hubbub.
It sounds like someone trying to talk
while blowing a big gum bubble.

Today, there was a hubbub.
I put the stolen page on the door to the front office
when I had a hall pass for the bathroom.

Then it was B lunch
and everyone saw it.

Who is doing this?
the kids ask with a laugh.
The teachers ask with dragon breath.

I'm not telling.

A ferocious temper! Never kind!
Most savage muzzle!
The battle did not end fairly.
The elder, old leader was beset
by the merciless fangs... of a boy!!!

The she-wolf had by now developed a ferocious temper. Her three suitors all bore the marks of her teeth. Yet they never replied in kind, never defended themselves against her. They turned their shoulders to her most savage slashes, and with wagging tails and mincing steps strove to placate her wrath. But if they were all mildness toward her, they were all fierceness toward one another. The three-year-old grew too ambitious in his fierceness. He caught the one-eyed elder on his blind side and ripped his ear into ribbons. Though the grizzled old fellow could see only on one side, against the youth and vigour of the other he brought into play the wisdom of long years of experience. His lost eye and his scarred muzzle bore evidence to the nature of his experience. He had survived too many battles to be in doubt for a moment about what to do.

The battle began fairly, but it did not end fairly. There was no telling what the outcome would have been, for the third wolf joined the elder, and together old leader and young leader, they attacked the ambitious three-year-old and proceeded to destroy him. He was beset on either side by the merciless fangs of his erstwhile comrades. Forgotten were the days they had hunted together, the game they had pulled down, the famine they had suffered. That business was a thing of the past. The business of love was at hand—ever a sterner and crueller business than that of food-getting.

And in the meanwhile, the she-wolf, the cause of it all, sat down contentedly on her haunches and watched. She was even pleased. This washer day—and it came not often—when man's bristled, and fang smote fang or ripped and tore the yielding flesh, all for the possession of her.

And in the business of love the three-year-old, who had made this his first adventure upon it, yielded up his life. On either side of his body stood his two rivals. They were gazing at the she-wolf, who sat smiling in the snow. But the elder leader was wise, very wise, in love even as in battle.

The younger leader turned his head to lick a wound on his shoulder. The curve of his neck was turned toward his rival. With his one eye the elder saw the opportunity. He darted in low and closed with his fangs. It was a long, ripping slash, and deep as well. His teeth, in passing, burst the wall of the great vein of the throat. Then he leaped clear.

The young leader snarled terribly, but his snarl broke midmost into a tickling cough. Bleeding and coughing, already stricken, he sprang at the elder and fought while life faded from him, his legs going weak beneath him, the light of day dulling on his eyes, his blows and springs falling shorter and shorter.

DAY 7

Late.
Petey's fault.
He was supposed to drop me off
in front.

Instead, I had to walk
six
whole
blocks
so he could take a shortcut
to Lacey's house.

Giant John was late, too,
which was good.

I had something soft to punch
to make my day
better.

Sort of.

• • • • •

Lacey Lacey Lacey
She's the only thing Petey
ever
ever
ever
talks about.

Unless he talks about his band
or how much he hates me,
which are both tied for his
second favorite
topic.

If Petey says
one
more
time
how lucky I am to be the baby
to get everything I want
I will smack him
even if he smacks harder.

I don't get everything I want.
I get nothing.
I get *Sort it out, boys!*

I get P*aul, help Kevin with his math.*
I get *My shift starts in 30 minutes,*
Petey will take you to school.

Doesn't Petey see?
I don't exist.

I had to walk six blocks
because of
Lacey Lacey Lacey
and get a tardy
and a detention for hitting Giant John
because of Petey.
Who is not—technically—the baby.
Anymore.

WEEKEND

There's this one channel with all the reruns.
It's my favorite.
It's where I met Cliff Huxtable.

Cliff Huxtable is a doctor
like my dad.
Delivers babies.
Has a bunch of kids.
But he's always home playing boring games
like chess
with his million kids.
My dad is NEVER home.
He never plays boring games.
Or any games.
He says that's just TV,
Dr. Huxtable being home all the time.
But you know what?
I don't care if it sounds stupid.
I wish TV was real.
And I don't even like chess.

• • • • •

Petey locked me in the bathroom
today.
He thought it was hilarious.
Yeah.
Funny.
I had to climb out the window.
And no one even noticed.

• • • • •

Petey and Philip.
Sixteen and seventeen.
Dumb as hammers.

Paul is almost out of here.
He wants to be a psychiatrist.
That means he asks a lot of annoying questions.

Patrick is the oldest.
He's in college and only comes home for
laundry.
And food.

That leaves me.
Kevin.
The baby.
The accident.

One college guy.
One senior.
One junior.
One sophomore.
And a seventh grader.
You can see how it might not work.

Paul says it could work.

It *should* work.

If my parents spent less time at work.

Maybe he's onto something.

Or maybe he's just annoying.

DAY 15

Give me that! Petey shouted
this morning in the car
on the way to school.
No, I said.
But he grabbed for it
swerving the car
just missing a fire hydrant.
NO! I said again,
but his arms are long
and his car is small.

That's why I'm writing this
on the back of old homework.
My notebook
is on the street
somewhere
because Petey is a moron
and says poetry is for old ladies.

• • • • •

By the way,
this isn't even poetry.
It's just thoughts
on paper
rapid fire
with not as many words
as usual thoughts
and none of those dumb
likes or as-es
or talking about trees
that old ladies like.
These are real thoughts
like a TV scroll
with a flow that's like a stream
that just flies out of my brain
like barf
but less gross.
Most of the time.

Wait.
Three *likes* just then.
Oh man.
Maybe this *is* poetry.
But cooler than regular poetry.

Yeah.

• • • • •

I'll walk home from school today
after detention.
No ride home in Petey's cruddy car.
I'll walk the whole 1.9 miles.
Maybe my notebook will still be in the road.
Or on the sidewalk.
Or in the grass.
Wherever it landed.
I didn't see.
Petey drives way too fast.

DAY 16

No luck.
The notebook is gone.
Or turned invisible.
I'm going to kill Petey.
When I get bigger than him.
Which might take a while.
Because he's like King Kong
with zits
and worse breath.

• • • • •

No one gets past me today.
I am a rock.
I am huge.
My face is stone
like those giant statues
from that one island
with giant face statues.

My island today:
the boys' bathroom
in the hallway outside the library.
No entry for dorks.

Unless they pay a toll
to the giant statue.

• • • • •

Robin in the hall,
so small compared to everyone.
He can sneak between them
unseen
like a bug.

But I see him.
I see what he's doing.
Freckle-Face Kelly's face is in flames,
Robin's hands flipping up her skirt.
She pushes him away
but she's too late.

Now everyone sees.
Her white, freckly legs.
Her white, flowery underpants.

And for just a second
I am moving fast.
I scatter the crowd
like a burst of bees exploding
when you hit their nest
with a rock.

Freckle-Face Kelly wipes her face.
Those little red spots don't smear
like you think they should.

She looks at me.
Robin looks at me.
Everyone looks at me.
Freckle-Face Kelly looks away first.
I think she wants to be stone, too.

In one move Robin is under my arm
kicking
yelling
but he can't sting me.
You can't sting stone.

. . . . .

Weenie Robin fits perfectly
under the sinks.

Toll paid.

He snaps right in
between the pipes
like a Lego
like he was made to fit there.

He's way noisier than a Lego, though
which is why Mrs. Little came
INTO
the boys' bathroom.

She is obviously
not a boy.

She is obviously
a librarian.

She is obviously
mad.

I am obviously
in trouble.

• • • • •

Mr. Hartwick is obviously
wearing an ugly tie.

Surprise.

• • • • •

Mrs. Little isn't even a teacher
so why can she send me to Hartwick?

Life's mysteries
abound.

• • • • •

Suspended.
A word that can describe medicine.
The little bits of healthy mold
suspended
in pink goo
so that the kids like the bits enough
to swallow them.

Suspended.
A word that can describe stopping
like someone hit a pause button and you are
suspended
in time and space
your finger frozen inches from your
nose.

Suspended.
A word that can describe
me.

• • • • •

You should have seen Mom's face
when she came to pick me up.
Not red.
Not purple.
No forehead veins,
like Hartwick's.

She just smiled really big.
I'll deal with him, she said
and then she laughed
but I know she wasn't really laughing.
Unless something
was funny
on her phone.

DAY 17

I dreamed about that smile last night
and woke up
shivering.

• • • • •

Mom hasn't talked to me
in 24 hours.
Dad is on call so he'll be back tomorrow.

Today is the first day
of three days
of not being allowed at school.

Is this what it means to be *dealt with*?
Isn't this sort of every kid's dream?
Missing parents.

No school.
Long weekend.
Is suspension really that big of a deal?

Paul says yes. It is a big deal.
But Paul never gets in trouble,
so how does he know?

• • • • •

The band is here tonight,
Petey and his friends
who all look the same.

They make sounds kind of like
the tornado did
but noisier
and less memorable.

Noisier Tornado.
That could be their band name.

DAY 19

I guess when you're suspended you're supposed to
think
about what you've done.

I am supposed to
think
shoving Robin under the sinks was
not cool.

I am supposed to
think
I'll never do anything like that
again.

You know what I really
think?

Petey shoves me under the sink
in the bathroom at home

All.
The.
Time.

No.
Big.
Deal.

No.
One.
Cares.

DAY 20

Get this.
As part of my punishment
Mom and Dad say Petey can't drive me
to school
anymore.

If I had known these were the
severe consequences
I'd face
I would have gotten suspended
a lot
sooner.

WEEKEND

Intervention.
That's what Paul called it.
He's taking a nighttime college class.
It's for nerds who want to be psychiatrists.
It teaches them words like "intervention."

When he said it, I thought he meant for me
but he meant for Petey.

He took Petey aside
while Petey rolled his eyes.
Paul told him to be a better big brother,
a better person.

Paul is the only one who sees Petey
as he is,
a King Kong jerk.

You'd think
Philip would see the King Kong jerk part, too—
but Philip is too busy
with football and girls
to notice anything
other than cheerleaders or boobs.

Paul told Petey to *watch it*.
Petey said *Watch THIS*.
And then punched a wall.

Paul rumpled my hair.
I think my getting suspended bothered Paul
more than anyone else.

More than
me.

DAY 23

Well.
My notebook is not lost.
Guess who found it?

Shrimpy Robin.

His face is like a dog
with a juicy bone.

Whatever.

• • • • •

No one can hear your heart beat fast
when you are jagged stone.

• • • • •

Mrs. Little put 50 pounds of books
in my arms.
Shelve them, she said.
Her mouth was tight,
puckered
like a cat
('s
butt).

This is part of the punishment.
Not just suspension.
Becoming Mrs. Little's slave
for two weeks
after school.

So boring
I might
die.

DAY 24

I did not die.
But now I might.

Robin made copies of some pages from my
notebook.
COPIES.

Gave them to everyone.
EVERYONE.

Guess who's going to get to watch his nose
EXPLODE OFF HIS FACE?

• • • • •

At least Robin didn't copy my secret
about messing up the books.
And at least he didn't copy Petey's crying secret.
Even with Petey in high school
he would still find out
from someone's big mouth.
I'm sure of it.

So now I'm worried
because Robin knows my secrets.
And I know he knows.
And he knows I know he knows.
And the way his smile curls like the Grinch
is no good.
That I know for sure.

• • • • •

Deep breaths.
Jagged stone turns to smooth rock.
Cold rock.
Rocks don't die.
Rocks have no feelings.
Rocks don't care.

• • • • •

Mrs. Little relaxed her cat-butt mouth
as she made me dust
the computers.

Your face is as white as a sheet, Kevin, she said.
Are you quite well?
Mrs. Little is from England.
She hardly ever talks.
But when she does,
sometimes she talks with extra words.

I didn't say anything
in case I threw up on the computers
and then had to clean it.

• • • • •

So much for being
cold rock
that doesn't care.

• • • • •

It turns out the problem with
having been suspended
is that you are not just on
thin ice,
as they say,
you have been sucked into
zero tolerance
which is like
zero gravity
except instead of floating in space
suspended,
you are pinned against a wall.
Frozen.
One misstep
and you're done.

• • • • •

I told Paul about the zero tolerance
and how I can't hit Robin
for making copies of my notebook
even though Robin could use a swift kick in the butt.

Paul said it's my own fault.
He said Robin is protected from me
because of me.

I don't know what that means
other than that Paul is annoying.

DAY 25

Poetry boy.
You'd think they could come up with something
better.

Poetry boy! Poetry boy!
Who's so tough now?

Poetry boy! Poetry boy!
Where's your dress?

Poetry boy! Poetry boy!
Harry's out to get you now.

Why is *poetry boy* a bad thing
when everyone loves the pages I put on the
walls?

Isn't that like poetry, too?
Messing with sentences to make new ones?

I'm no boy. I'm an outlaw.
I'm a poetry *bandit.*

Maybe I should tell my secret.
Spill the beans.

Except what about zero tolerance?
What about MAJOR CONSEQUENCES, MISTER?

It's all so dumb.
It doesn't bother me.

Poetry boy! Poetry boy!
Whatever.

• • • • •

Robin is their leader.
By the way.

He thinks I'm easy prey
as he leads the chants
with his juicy dog-bone face.

That I can't hit.
Anymore.

DAY 26

Robin says he'll tell on me.
He'll tell everyone I'm the one
who puts the marked-up pages on the walls
and I'll be in big trouble
because of the zero tolerance thing.

But

He'll keep my secret safe if I do one thing.
He wants me to mark up the pages
and then HE wants to put them on the walls.

HE wants to be the outlaw.
The Poetry Bandit.

Hmph.

I don't care.
I don't.
Really.

• • • • •

I told him he'll get in trouble.
He says no he won't.
I told him those are my bandit words.
He says not anymore.
I said I won't do it.
He says he'll make sure I get in trouble for it, then.
He'll make sure everyone sees my whole notebook, too.
All of it.
I'll be murdered by Petey
and then I'll be expelled.

This is a problem.

• • • • •

They all loved it, of course.
Well, except for the teachers.
But no one cares about them.

Now Robin wants me to "discover" him,
so he can be King of the School for real.
That made me laugh.
"King of the School" is not an actual thing.
(But it would be a good band name.)

I was just making fun of him.
Duh.

You're dreadfully ignorant
if you have thought I am not
King of this school!

64

Then Wendy saw the shadow on the floor, looking so draggled, and she was frightfully sorry for Peter. "How awful!" she said, but she could not help smiling when she saw that he had been trying to stick it on with soap. How exactly like a boy!

Fortunately she knew at once what to do. "It must be sewn on," she said, just a little patronisingly.

"What's sewn?" he asked.

"You're dreadfully ignorant."

"No, I'm not."

But she was exulting in his ignorance. "I shall sew it on for you, my little man," she said, though he was tall as herself, and she got out her housewife [sewing bag], and sewed the shadow on to Peter's foot.

"I daresay it will hurt a little," she warned him.

"Oh, I shan't cry," said Peter, who was already of the opinion that he had never cried in his life. And he clenched his teeth and did not cry, and soon his shadow was behaving properly, though still a little creased.

"Perhaps I should have ironed it," Wendy said thoughtfully, but Peter, boylike, was indifferent to appearances, and he was now jumping about in the wildest glee. Alas, he had already forgotten that he owed his bliss to Wendy. He thought he had attached the shadow himself. "How clever I am!" he crowed rapturously, "oh, the cleverness of me!"

It is humiliating to have to confess that this conceit of Peter was one of his most fascinating qualities. To put it with brutal frankness, there never was a cockier boy.

But for the moment Wendy was shocked. "You conceit [braggart]," she exclaimed, with frightful sarcasm; "of course I did nothing!"

"You did a little," Peter said carelessly, and continued to dance.

"A little!" she replied with hauteur [pride]; "if I am no use I can at least withdraw," and she sprang in the most dignified way into bed and covered her face with the blankets.

To induce her to look up he pretended to be going away, and when this failed he sat on the end of the bed and tapped her gently with his foot. "Wendy," he said, "don't withdraw. I can't help crowing, Wendy, when I'm pleased with myself." Still she would not look up, though she was listening eagerly. "Wendy," he continued, in a voice that no woman has ever yet been able to resist, "Wendy, one girl is more use than twenty boys."

Now Wendy was every inch a woman, though there were not very many inches,

DAY 9,342

It's not really day 9,342.
But it feels like it.

Shelving books.
Poetry boy.
Poetry boy.
Shelving books.
Poetry boy.
Poetry boy.
Shelving books.

The days don't even separate anymore.
It is all just one long
never
end
ing
day.

• • • • •

The Cat Stranglers.
That should be Petey's band's name.
Or Cat Tornadoes
or Bleeding Ears
or Bleeding Cat Tornado Ears.
Something like that.

I don't know what they're doing in there
but it doesn't sound like music.
What they need is a real song,
real words
to scream
in that microphone.

We hate everybody!
We hate you!
We hate everybody!
Especially you!
We hate everybody!
We hate you!
We hate everybody!
We scream till we're blue!

See? That wasn't hard.

DAY I DON'T EVEN KNOW ANYMORE

Metamorphosis.
We watched a movie about it in science.

It's when a caterpillar snuggles up in a chrysalis
like a backward mummy.

Instead of dying and being wrapped up,
it wraps itself up to live.
To become something new,
something with freedom.
Something pretty.

Unless it's a moth.
A moth still has freedom,
but it's
Ugly
Gross
Brown
Dusty.

It's just a dirty moth.

In that case, metamorphosis is kind of sad.
Little caterpillar wraps itself up
like a kid in elementary school
going to sleep
and waking up a pizza-faced middle school weirdo.

Robin is changing, growing wings
every day
in a chrysalis made of my notebook.
A revenge chrysalis.
(Which would be a good name for a band.)

If I squint, I can see his
Ugly
Gross
Dusty
Dirty
moth wings.
His pizza face.
His pale eyes
glowing with greed
at the laughs he gets
at my expense
that Mrs. Smithson ignores.

Just like fake moth eyes on ugly wings
Robin's eyes
better be hiding
his true self—
that he is still scared of me.
Because he should be.

WEEKEND

Dad asked what was going on.
But he meant it like,
Hey, bro! What's going on?
Like a dude punching another dude's shoulder
at the beach.

So I said:
Nothing

Because that's what he wanted me to say.

• • • • •

If I am made of stone at home
no one can bother me.

If I am made of stone at school
no one can bother me.

Paul says even stones have to crack
to let out steam.

But what he doesn't understand is that
there is always someone
who wants to stick their head in a crack
and sniff around.

Hahaha.

But seriously.
Paul is so annoying.

DAY 30-SOMETHING

Hartwick was looking at me
from his office across the hall.
I wanted to say
You can't look at me like that.
I wanted to say
Hide those beady eyes back under your greasy lids.
I wanted to say
Go away.
But I didn't say anything
because the nurse was putting antiseptic on my lip
where it busted open
after I fell on it
in the hallway
when Robin tripped me
and said
*Poetry boy can't write sentences
or walk, either.*
And Giant John laughed.

• • • • •

It's a shame, really,
how Mrs. Smithson ignores Robin
as he seeks revenge.

She is depriving him
of the ceiling stain
of Hartwick's tie-nightmare-of-the-day
of the SHOUTING ABOUT RESPONSIBILITY.

The moth-faced boy flies free.
Again.

• • • • •

My heartbeat in my lip.
Mom pinched her face up tight.
She made sure I didn't need stitches.

Philip high-fived me
when I said *You should've seen the other guy.*
Petey just rolled his eyes
and Paul sighed real big.

But there was no other guy.
Unless you count Robin
looking innocent
as Mrs. Smithson and Harry
bobbled by.

• • • • •   ·

Robin says it's time for another Poetry Bandit
thing.

I told him to go rip out a page from the library.
He said no, that I should do it.

Blackmail stinks.
(Another good band name.)

• • • • •

I put it up before I gave it to Robin.
I think he grew three inches just from being mad.
He wanted to get "caught" putting it up,
by me.
I told him to go sign his name if he wants all the credit.
But someone had already thrown it away.

The teachers, they learn fast.

She is a great [huge] ugly girl!
She can't be a lady!
She is a MONSTER TEACHER.
We despise her. ♋➤

He had to translate. "She is not very polite. She says you are a great [huge] ugly girl, and that she is my fairy."

He tried to argue with Tink. "You know you can't be my fairy, Tink, because I am a gentleman and you are a lady."

To this Tink replied in these words, "You silly ass," and disappeared into the bathroom. "She is quite a common fairy," Peter explained apologetically, "she is called Tinker Bell because she mends the pots and kettles [tinker = tin worker]." [Similar to "cinder" plus "elle" to get Cinderella.]

They were together in the armchair by this time, and Wendy plied him with more questions.

"If you don't live in Kensington Gardens now—"

"Sometimes I do still."

"But where do you live mostly?"

"With the lost boys."

"Who are they?"

"They are the children who fall out of their perambulators when the nurse is looking the other way. If they are not claimed in seven days they are sent far away to the Neverland to defray expenses. I'm captain."

"What fun it must be!"

"Yes," said cunning Peter, "but we are rather lonely. You see we have no female companionship."

"Are none of the others girls?"

"Oh, no; girls, you know, are much too clever to fall out of their prams."

This flattered Wendy immensely. "I think," she said, "it is perfectly lovely the way you talk about girls; John there just despises us."

For reply Peter rose and kicked John out of bed, blankets and all; one kick. This seemed to Wendy rather forward for a first meeting, and she told him with spirit that he was not captain in her house. However, John continued to sleep so placidly on the floor that she allowed him to remain there. "And I know you meant to be kind," she said, relenting, "so you may give me a kiss."

For the moment she had forgotten his ignorance about kisses. "I thought you

Peter Pan

TUESDAY

Mrs. Little looks at me sideways.
I know she wants to say something
but I don't want to listen
so I pretend I don't see
her eyes
in the corner of her face
like a hieroglyph.

• • • • •

It's not like I never had a fat lip.
That's what I want to say
to her hieroglyph eye.

Every time I look up and see her
she is staring.
And she doesn't look away.
It's like she wants me to see.

She's looking, searching, telling me something
that I can't hear.

Just like my lip keeps a beat
to a song I can't hear.

• • • • •

I'm glad for the books today,
heavy in my hands.
They go on the shelves,
one after the other.
I don't have to think.
I don't want to think.
Building a fortress
of books
all around me.

• • • • •

I worked for an hour before I realized
today is Tuesday.
The day after
my library detentions ended.

WEDNESDAY

Rocks don't eat lunch.
Rocks don't eat at all.
Rocks don't hide from moth boys
bent on revenge.

But I'm hungry.

• • • • •

Ham sandwich in my backpack.
Left the chips at home.
Too noisy.
If I sit back by the old encyclopedias
Mrs. Little doesn't see me,
or pretends like she doesn't see me,
and I can eat in peace.
No one spilling milk on my food
"accidentally."
No one saying
Roses are red
Violets are purple
Kevin writes poems
Because he's a girl

That's a terrible poem
by the way.

Though "girple" would be an awesome word.

• • • • •

Tried to leave the library
but Mrs. Little tapped me on the arm.
Her cat-butt face
was in full force
but her eyes were softer.
Maybe.

I've seen what you've done to the books,
she whispered.
I'm aware of your little schemes.
She sounded like she was a ghost
from England.

I pulled my arm away and ran
trying to disappear like I was a ghost
from Busted-ville.

• • • • •

The noise again.
Maybe that should be the band's name.
Just . . .
The Noise.

They make their screeches and whines
like robot animals fighting to the death.
Today I scream with them:

I feel lost all the time
A toy in a shoe
A sock in the trash
What do I do?

The boy who is lost
Though they see me right here
I cannot be found
But I can't disappear.

Until Petey comes to my room
and tells me to shut up.
Your dumb rhymes are ruining the music, he says,
and I want to laugh
but it sticks in my throat
because ruining things
seems to be my new specialty.

THURSDAY

The Poetry Bandit is in trouble.

Mrs. Little knows it's me.
Robin knows it's me.

Robin wants it to be him.
So he can be King of the School.

Am I going to be King of the School now?
I highly doubt it.

I don't think you can be king
if you're expelled.

• • • • •

I put this one on Mrs. Little's desk.
So maybe she'll know
why I hurt
the books.

Fighting for some way of escape.
It's no use! I should have saw
mine coming! ·· ➡

The players all played at once without waiting for turns, quarrelling all the while, and fighting for the hedgehogs; and in a very short time the Queen was in a furious passion, and went stamping about, and shouting "Off with his head!" or "Off with her head!" about once in a minute.

Alice began to feel very uneasy: to be sure, she had not as yet had any dispute with the Queen, but she knew that it might happen any minute, "and then," thought she, "what would become of me? They're dreadfully fond of beheading people here; the great wonder is, that there's any one left alive!"

She was looking about for some way of escape, and wondering whether she could get away without being seen, when she noticed a curious appearance in the air: it puzzled her very much at first, but, after watching it a minute or two, she made it out to be a grin, and she said to herself "It's the Cheshire Cat: now I shall have somebody to talk to."

"How are you getting on?" said the Cat, as soon as there was mouth enough for it to speak with.

Alice waited till the eyes appeared, and then nodded. "It's no use speaking to it," she thought, 'till its ears have come, or at least one of them." In another minute the whole head appeared, and then Alice put down her flamingo, and began an account of the game, feeling very glad she had someone to listen to her. The Cat seemed to think that there was enough of it now in sight, and no more of it appeared.

"I don't think they play at all fairly," Alice began, in rather a complaining tone, "and they all quarrel so dreadfully one can't hear oneself speak—and they don't seem to have any rules in particular; at least, if there are, nobody attends to them—and you've no idea how confusing it is all the things being alive, for instance, there's the arch I've got to go through next walking about at the other end of the ground—and I should have croqueted the Queen's hedgehog just now, only it ran away when it saw mine coming!"

Alice in Wonderland

• • • • •

The intercom buzzed in Social Studies,
and in front of everyone
it was announced:
Please send Kevin Jamison to Mr. Hartwick's office.
Ooooh.
Giggle.
Yeeeer in truhhhhbullll.
Harry the mole bounced at Freckle-Face Kelly and Robin,
of course,
to walk me to the office.

Buddy system.

Not.

• • • • •

Water on my pants.
Well, not just my pants . . .
my crotchal area.

Thanks to gum on the water fountain.
Gum I didn't see.

Robin almost passed out from laughing.
I almost passed out from not punching him.

• • • • •

Luckily Robin doesn't know why I was called
to see Hartwick.

All his Poetry Bandit dreams
down the drain.

I can still hear him laughing
while I sit in the office.
Yeah, well,
we'll see who laughs last.

At least Freckle-Face Kelly didn't laugh.

I mean, *Kelly* didn't laugh.

• • • • •

The stain on the ceiling again,
in the shape of a cauliflower.
The stain fills my pupils
my brain
my ears
instead of Hartwick and Mrs. Little's words
discussing my fate
for defacing school property.

In my defense, I did not remove any faces from
anything.

I stare at the stain
and congratulate it in my head
for getting bigger since we've seen each other last.

• • • • •

Two more weeks' detention.
In the library.
Not expelled!
But I'm on THIN ICE
Hartwick says. His favorite thing to say.
And I totter, in my head, on the brink
of a lake paved with icy poems cracking under
my feet.
YOUNG MAN
Purple veins pulse to get my attention.
LAST CHANCE
Fingers shake at me.
OUT OF HERE
Mrs. Little stands and so I do, too.
THIN ICE
Repeated
Ringing in my ears
Thin ice
Thin ice
Thin ice

• • • • •

As a side note,
I have composed an ode
to Hartwick's tie:

[Clearing throat noise here]

O, Principal's tie
You make me want to scream
Because you are the color of
Puked-up Neapolitan ice cream

• • • • •

Why did Mrs. Little have to tell?
Her eyes seem to like me.
Her ears seem to hear me.
Why would she want me in trouble?

Maybe she's lonely
in the big library
all by herself.
Maybe she needs company.

I don't really mind being here, though.
Even if she stares at me
with her hieroglyph eye.

There are no sabotaged water fountains
in the library.

FRIDAY

I tried to explain better
about everything.

It will probably backfire
again.

I ripped this one out of a book
from home.

Once a child had great power
and was dreaded by all the world!
Then he let himself down again.
He was terribly afraid. A thief
suffering terror the name of ⟹
~~Kevin~~ Robin. ⟹

Rapunzel

There were once a man and a woman who had long in vain wished for a child. At length the woman hoped that God was about to grant her desire.

These people had a little window at the back of their house from which a splendid garden could be seen, which was full of the most beautiful flowers and herbs. It was, however, surrounded by a high wall, and no one dared to go into it because it belonged to an enchantress, who had great power and was dreaded by all the world.

One day the woman was standing by this window and looking down into the garden, when she saw a bed which was planted with the most beautiful rampion (rapunzel), and it looked so fresh and green that she longed for it, she quite pined away, and began to look pale and miserable.

Then her husband was alarmed, and asked: "What ails you, dear wife?"

"Ah," she replied, "if I can't eat some of the rampion, which is in the garden behind our house, I shall die."

The man, who loved her, thought: "Sooner than let your wife die, bring her some of the rampion yourself, let it cost what it will."

At twilight, he clambered down over the wall into the garden of the enchantress, hastily clutched a handful of rampion, and took it to his wife. She at once made herself a salad of it, and ate it greedily. It tasted so good to her—so very good, that the next day she longed for it three times as much as before.

If he was to have any rest, her husband must once more descend into the garden. In the gloom of evening therefore, he let himself down again; but when he had clambered down the wall he was terribly afraid, for he saw the enchantress standing before him.

"How can you dare," said she with angry look, "descend into my garden and steal my rampion like a thief? You shall suffer for it!"

"Ah," answered he, "let mercy take the place of justice, I only made up my mind to do it out of necessity. My wife saw your rampion from the window, and felt such a longing for it that she would have died if she had not got some to eat."

Then the enchantress allowed her anger to be softened, and said to him: "If the case be as you say, I will allow you to take away with you as much rampion as you will, only I make one condition, you must give me the child which your wife will bring into the world; it shall be well treated, and I will care for it like a mother."

The man in his terror consented to everything, and when the woman was brought to bed, the enchantress appeared at once, gave the child the name of Rapunzel, and took it away with her.

~~Kevin~~ Robin

• • • • •

She makes me explain what I meant.
So I do.

You've got yourself in a bind, then.
She looks at me over her glasses.

I nod.

Just tell him you've been caught, Kevin.
His Poetry Bandit machinations can go no further.

I don't know what that means.
Except that she still doesn't understand.

• • • • •

My hand on the door,
it vibrates with the robot murder noises.
The KEEP OUT sign shakes a little, too.

Today I yell into my invisible microphone:

Rumbling, stumbling, fumbling, crumbling
but there is nowhere to go.
I've become easy prey
and there is nowhere to go.

Go! Go! Go! Go!
Go! Go! Go! Go!

But I've become easy prey
and there is nowhere to go—

The door yanks open, Petey is sweaty,
his eyes black arrows, stabbing at my face.

Get away from my door
you creeper.

Hey man,
the one friend says,
the guy who looks like all the rest of them.
His rhymes are kind of maybe not half bad.

Petey's hand goes to the middle of my chest,
his palm against my shirt.
He pushes.
I stumble back.
Get out of here, turd!
And he slams the door.

But I smile.
Because I'm kind of maybe not half bad.

MONDAY

398 GR
This is the section for fairy tales.
Not the section for a random photocopied page
flittering around
making a mess.

I take the loose page to the trash,
but then I see
the page has the word
"wolf"
circled in red.

Like an invitation.

LATER MONDAY

I put my poem on a shelf
with the poetry books.

Hopefully Mrs. Little will find it there.
Properly shelved.

And maybe she will understand.

Wolf! You do not hear
how sweet the wolf
can be. ⟶

Red Riding-Cap

The wolf thought to himself, "What a tender young creature! what a nice plump mouthful—she will be better to eat than the old woman. I must act craftily, so as to catch both."

So he walked for a short time by the side of Little Red-Cap, and then he said: "See, Little Red-Cap, how pretty the flowers are about here—why do you not look round? I believe too, that you do not hear how sweetly the little birds are singing; you walk gravely along as if you were going to school, while everything else out here in the wood is merry."

Little Red-Cap raised her eyes, and when she saw the sunbeams dancing here and there through the trees, and pretty flowers growing everywhere, she thought, "Suppose I take grandmother a fresh nosegay; that would please her too. It is so early in the day that I shall still get there in good time;" and so she ran from the path into the wood to look for flowers. And whenever she had picked one, she fancied that she saw a still prettier one farther on, and ran after it, and so got deeper and deeper into the wood.

Meanwhile the wolf ran straight to the grandmother's house and knocked at the door.

"Who is there?"

"Little Red-Cap," replied the wolf. "She is bringing cake and wine; open the door."

"Lift the latch," called out the grandmother, "I am too weak, and cannot get up."

The wolf lifted the latch, the door flew open, and without saying a word he went straight to the grandmother's bed, and devoured her. Then he put on her clothes, dressed himself in her cap, laid himself in bed and drew the curtains.

Little Red-Cap, however, had been running about picking flowers, and when she had gathered so many that she could carry no more, she remembered her grandmother, and set out on the way to her.

She was surprised to find the cottage-door standing open, and when she went into the room, she had such a strange feeling that she said to herself, "Oh dear! how uneasy I feel to-day, and at other times I like being with grandmother so much." She called out, "Good morning," but received no answer; so she went to the bed and drew back the curtains. There lay her grandmother with her cap pulled far over her face, and looking very strange.

"Oh! grandmother," she said, "what big ears you have!"

"All the better to hear you with, my child," was the reply.

"But, grandmother, what big eyes you have!" she said.

TUESDAY

I

On my desk this morning,
a familiar page
copied from a familiar notebook
about a familiar topic
having to do with a familiar mole
on a familiar teacher's face.

II

ON EVERY DESK,
a familiar page
copied from a familiar notebook
about a familiar topic
having to do with a familiar mole
on a familiar teacher's face.

III

On Robin's moth face,
a familiar look
copied from a familiar face
I used to see in a familiar mirror
when I was stuffing a familiar someone
under the familiar sinks.

IV

Stolen a page from your own book, hmm?
That was Mrs. Smithson.
She actually said it.
In her familiar voice.
Out loud.
Before she grabbed most of the papers
and recycled them.

• • • • •

I am not a stone.
I am not a rock.
I am not giant and unblinking and cold.
There is an earthquake.
In my guts.
Shaking and quaking.
Quaking and shaking.
Cracking and jagged.
Jagged and cracking.
Breaking everything into sharp points,
poking my insides
until I want to scream.
But instead, I put my head on my desk
and close my eyes slowly
and wonder how the earthquake in my guts
isn't shaking the whole classroom.

• • • • •

Kelly looks at me.
Her head is on her desk, too.
Those freckles are the same color as the desk,
like the desk has splashed a little on her face.

She blinks.

I blink.

She slides the paper into her lap,
the paper with my Harry poem.
She crumples it and drops it on the floor.

She smiles.

I stare.

One side of my mouth twitches up.
It's hard to smile with so many
jagged places.

THURSDAY

001.94
Not the poetry section,
the mystery section.
But there's a book misshelved.
A book with poems and quotes
short and funny
that go off like firecrackers in my brain
surprising me
until I laugh and laugh
for the first time in days and days.
And I see her smile,
Mrs. Little behind the checkout desk,
not looking up.

I put my poem in the book
and put the book on the right shelf
with the other poems.

Maybe Mrs. Little will find it
like I found her misshelved book.

And maybe she will laugh
with fireworks in her brain.

LATER THURSDAY

Better to be
~~a witty fool~~ A BRAINY TURD
than
~~a foolish wit.~~ A TURD-LIKE BRAIN

-~~shakespeare~~
KEVIN

FRIDAY

Instead of chasing Kelly
or punching Giant John like pizza dough
I try to be Godzilla
to Robin's Mothra.
I am bigger
but he is suddenly meaner.
My words, in my notebook
have given him power over me
which isn't fair.

Paul would say it *is* kind of fair,
in a karma kind of way.
But never forget
Paul is annoying.

I see the library window from the recess field.
Maybe I could go there
like Godzilla in the ocean.
Regenerate my powers.

But no.
Robin and I shout at each other,
shooting fire from our mouths.
Angry enemies.

He still wants to be the Poetry Bandit.
He still wants all the credit.

When I get close to his face
the fire from my mouth to his ear
burns the truth in his head.

Mrs. Little knows about me and the books.
Hartwick knows about me and the books.

The Poetry Bandit has been discovered.
The Poetry Bandit is done.

• • • • •

Like a moth to flame
I lure Robin in with my tractor beam of words.
I call him all the worst things:
A baby. A jealous nerd. Ugly.
But he is word-proof now, a fireproof moth.
He does not combust.
He expands.
Kevin, Kevin, poetry boy, he yells.
Kevin has 900 brothers who all hate him.
Kevin has no friends.
Robin grows ten times bigger than my Godzilla.
Swollen with angry revenge.

• • • • •

Kelly grabs my hand
in the middle of the shouting fight
with Robin.

My face catches on fire.

She drags me off. She says,
Maybe if you apologize to him, he'll stop.
And I say,
Bluh, whugh, huh blerf
because she's still holding my hand.

• • • • •

808.51
Not the poetry section.
Again.
I smile.
There is a note.
A flyer.
I unfold it as if it is a treasure map,
or a secret message from the FBI.

Instead, it is an announcement.
Beatnik's Brews
Poetry Night
Friday
8 pm
And a handwritten note:
If your parents give permission, I can give you a ride.

I look at the checkout desk
and think about the silver car with a dent
that I sometimes see Mrs. Little climb into
after school.
I wonder if it smells funny in that car.
If the AC works.
What music scrambles from the speakers.

Mrs. Little glances up
over her half-rectangle glasses
and
smiles.

The light catches the diamonds
on the sides of her glasses
or the fake diamonds
or whatever.

Her whole face is sparkly,
and for just a speck of a second
I see what she looked like
when she wasn't 9,000 years old.

I smile back.

●　●　●　●　●

I put my poem in the book,
and put the book on the right shelf
with the other poems.

Maybe Mrs. Little will find it
like I found her folded flyer.

And maybe she'll smile
at the words I wrote.

BEATNIK'S BREWS
POETRY NIGHT

BRAIN BLOWS A FUSE!

If your parents give permission, I can give you a ride.

FRIGHT!

Come share your best (or worst) work at

Friday's open mic night. All ages welcome.

Craz-ay!

Poetry slammin' starts at 8. ←

LATE PM!

Be there or be square!

LATER FRIDAY

I don't sing anything myself today.
Instead I slide a paper under the door
and run fast to my room
before Petey can call me a turd.

SATURDAY

Football on TV.
Somehow the whole family is home.
A packed house.
Even Patrick, home from college for the weekend.

Paul and I on the floor,
cheering.
Dad throws chips at us.
He is laughing.
Wrong team! he yells
and we know it
which is why we cheer.

Mom reads a book,
her feet in Dad's lap.
Petey and Philip call plays
before the announcer says them.

Patrick is in the kitchen
eating all the food.

We are a real family.
Like a TV show,

but a classy one
with a live audience laugh track.

• • • • •

I make it a rule
to not think about school when I'm at home.
But I can't help wonder
What kind of TV show does Robin live in?
What kind of TV show does Kelly live in?
What kind of TV show does Mrs. Little live in?
Do they have live audience laugh tracks?
A chorus of "awww"s?
I bet Mrs. Little has a funny theme song
running through her show,
that seems simple,
but then busts out with bongos.
Always a surprise.

• • • • •

Mom doesn't look up from her book.
She says,
Oh yeah, Friday we're all going to dinner
together
with my boss.
Dad's eyebrows go up like helium-filled
caterpillars.
Paul says, *Everyone?*
Everyone.
Petey says, *Can I bring Lacey?*
No.
The game comes back on.
I think no one hears when I say,
But I have plans.
Then Petey and Philip bust out laughing.
Got a hot date?
Got a bank to rob?
Now everyone joins in.
Job interview?
Skydiving?
Bus driving lessons?

They're hilarious.

Not.

Everyone needs to be there, Kevin.
Mom's face goes pointy.
This could mean a promotion for me.
Normal hours.
More money.
Everything we all want.
So everyone comes. On their best behavior.

Everyone.

MONDAY

Hansel and Gretel

The two children had also not been able to sleep for hunger, and had heard what their stepmother had said to their father. Gretel wept bitter tears, and said to Hansel: "Now all is over with us." "Be quiet, Gretel," said Hansel, "do not distress yourself, I will soon find a way to help us." And when the old folks had fallen asleep, he got up, put on his little coat, opened the door below, and crept outside. The moon shone brightly, and the white pebbles which lay in front of the house glittered like real silver pennies. Hansel stooped and stuffed the little pocket of his coat with as many as he could get in. Then he went back and said to Gretel: "Be comforted, dear little sister, and sleep in peace, God will not forsake us," and he lay down again in his bed. When day dawned, but before the sun had risen, the woman came and awoke the two children, saying: "Get up, you sluggards! we are going into the forest to fetch wood." She gave each a little piece of bread, and said: "There is something for your dinner, but do not eat it up before then, for you will get nothing else." Gretel took the bread under her apron, as Hansel had the stones in his pocket. Then they all set out together on the way to the forest. When they had walked a short time, Hansel stood still and peeped back at the house, and did so again and again. His father said: "Hansel, what are you looking at there and staying behind for? Pay attention, and do not forget how to use your legs." "Ah, father," said Hansel, "I am looking at my little white cat, which is sitting up on the roof, and wants to say goodbye to me." The wife said: "Fool, that is not your little cat, that is the morning sun which is shining on the chimneys." Hansel, however, had not been looking back at the cat, but had been constantly throwing one of the white pebble-stones out of his pocket on the road.

I put it on the shelving cart,
and then I leave.

TUESDAY

Old lady hand on my shoulder.
Veins and wrinkles,
shiny rings,
but when I close my eyes
energy shoots from the veins
like from a superhero
whose power is to say
That's okay,
but without using words.

• • • • •

There are people who talk
so much
all the time
forever
with words falling from their mouths
like crumbs
from a sandwich.

But then there are people who never talk
hardly ever.
Except with their eyes
and their head-tilts
and their lips that can smile and frown
at the same time.

Mrs. Little says so much
without ever
ever
SHOUTING ABOUT RESPONSIBILITY.

THURSDAY

Do you think Kevin is a stupid loser?
That's what the note said
in perfect handwriting
though the paper was so wrinkled
it looked like my Easter shirt
wadded up at the bottom of my drawer.

Robin tossed it on my chair.
(The note, not my Easter shirt.)
A big box was checked
YES
Everyone signed it. Everyone except Kelly.
Someone even pretended to sign Mrs. Smithson's name.
At least I'm pretty sure it was fake.

Harry the mole signed it, too.

• • • • •

Eyes on me
is all she says.
Not *Don't pass notes, Robin.*
Not *See me after class, Robin.*
Not *Pay attention, Robin.*

Eyes on me.
How can eyes NOT be on her
with Harry staring at us like that?

• • • • •

My pillow over my head.
My homework on the floor.
My window painted shut.
My door closed with a chair under the knob.
No one in.
No one out.
I breathe into the pillow, hot breath stinking it up.
Then I hear it.
Muffled.

The pillow hits the floor.
The homework is under my foot.
The window blinds rattle.
The chair goes back to the desk.
I am in the hall.
I am out.

Because I think I heard something.
Something I could not possibly have heard.
But then I hear it again.
Among the robot cat-slaughter sounds.

The days go by so long and so hard
The days go by so slow and so far
The days go by so stretched like a chord
From broken-down, slammed-around electric guitars

My words.
Coming from the guy who looks like the other guys.
They saw my paper.
They're singing my rhymes.

I am so happy I punch the air.
And it feels better
than punching Giant John
ever did.

FRIDAY

It doesn't make sense that wearing a necktie
could make a difference
at all
in the world
ever,
but especially when it comes to my mom
getting a promotion.
And yet, I am strangled by blue with small red dots
the same colors my face will be
any minute now.

• • • • •

I didn't want to see poetry readings anyway.
Fancy people onstage
talking about flowers and trees
and ravens and feelings.
I don't care
about any of that stuff.

Jagged rocks don't care about people onstage.
Jagged rocks don't care about flowers.
Jagged rocks don't have feelings.

Except maybe they do.
Except maybe I do.

• • • • •

I.
Hate.
This.
Tie.

DINNER

You know how when something bad happens
your ears feel stuffed with socks,
your eyes focus like microscopes,
your cheeks catch on fire,
time slows down,
and no matter how much you
wish
pray
promise
beg
a hole does not open up and swallow you?

Well, none of that changes
when you're at a fancy restaurant
with your mom's boss
and your brother
puts Tabasco sauce on your fries
and you don't notice until it's too late
so you punch him under the table
while you're choking and gasping
and spitting French fry chunks
everywhere.

And you knock your drink
into your mom's boss's drink
like dominoes
that land in his lap,
but cold and wet
and smelling
like the lady who works at the post office.

FRIDAY NEVER ENDS

Mom is so angry.
Maybe angrier than ever before.
I can see it in her face.
The way her eyes don't match the curl of her lips.
The way her eyes suck in all the energy of the room.
The way her eyes are a vortex
trying to swallow me whole.

FRIDAY NEVER ENDS. THE OUTSIDE OF THE RESTAURANT EDITION

The bench is hard and the metal hurts my back
but it's better out here than inside
listening to Mom apologize for me.
Always the mistake.
Always ruining things.

• • • • •

I kick a rock out from under the bench.
It hits a trash can, and with a *BANG*,
it breaks in half.
Good.

• • • • •

I sit in the night for a long time,
watching cars go by.
It stinks to live in a really small town,
because tonight I know all the cars.
Everyone seeing me on the bench,
a statue formerly known as Kevin.

• • • • •

Cars stop and go at the red light.
Customers come and go from the restaurant.
I shoot laser eyes at everyone.
Stop and go. *ZAP.*
Come and go. *ZAP.*
They're not trapped.
Like me.
Zap.

• • • • •

One car stops at the light even though it's green.
Two cars honk,
but it doesn't move.
I zap it with my laser eyes.
It still doesn't move.
It is an old car.
Beat up.
Silver.
With rust on the bottom.
Do I know this car, too?

• • • • •

In jerks, the passenger window opens
like the jerks I feel when I fall asleep,
only now I'm waking up
more and more
with each jerk of the window.

• • • • •

Kevin? Is that you?
The voice doesn't belong in the nighttime
or in the road
or between the honks
of other angry drivers.
I stand, my statue legs breaking free.
She has leaned across the seat to open the window,
her silver hair around her shoulders,
shining in the streetlights.
Shadows darken her wrinkles.
I walk to the sidewalk.
Hold up my hand
to wave hi
or say *Stop, please?*

• • • • •

What's the matter, then?
Her voice belongs in *The Sound of Music*
or on PBS
not in the parking lot of Chez Whatever.
It turns out I've been crying.
Who knew?
Her face is soft with sympathy. So soft I feel sick.
She puts her hand on my shoulder.
It makes me jump.
Kevin.
How can I help?
I hiccup. Wipe my face.
Where are your parents?

FRIDAY RESCUE

Wind on my face.
Seat belt on.
Tie off.
I am free.
For now.

• • • • •

She just walked in, like a queen.
Introduced herself,
apologized for interrupting,
asked if she could borrow me.
Dad couldn't say anything.
Mom tried to say no.
Mrs. Little wouldn't listen, though.
She called me talented.
A poet.
Paul ruffled my hair and smiled.
Philip and Petey snickered but Mom's boss gave them
LASER EYES
and they stopped.

She called me
A schemer, no doubt.
But also?
Smart.
Funny.
Fragile.
Dad's mouth stayed open
catching flies
if Chez Whatever
had flies.

Certainly, he should go,
Mom's boss said, standing, shaking Mrs. Little's hand,
his pants still wet.
You must be so proud,
he said to Mom, smiling.
Her face turned pink from the neck up,
a crawling warmth, climbing behind her ears
until she said with bright eyes,
Yes.
Yes, I am.

• • • • •

What?
She's giving me the hieroglyph eye as she drives.
What? she asks again.
I am giving her the hieroglyph eye back.

The words she just said in there . . .
so many
at one time.
More than I've ever heard her say.
And they were all about me.
And they were nice.

They didn't fall from her mouth.
They flew.
Like flaming arrows.
Flaming arrows keeping everyone away.
But keeping me warm.

What? She asks one more time,
Her hieroglyph eye shining in the dark.

Nothing, I say.
I hope my hieroglyph eye is shining, too.

OPEN MIC

How old is this guy?
His glasses say old,
but his shorts say young.
His words say old,
but his smile says young.
He talks in the microphone like he's telling a secret,
but we can all hear.

• • • • •

I drink a hot cup of decaf coffee.
It tastes like my dad's breath on Sundays.
Mrs. Little says
You can't watch an open mic without coffee.
but she smiles when I push mine away,
and she buys me a Coke
in a real glass bottle.

• • • • •

My eyes wide.
The girl said a swear right into the microphone.
No one seems to notice
except me.

• • • • •

A teacher in the night
at a table
in a coffee shop
like a regular person
is weird.

Like a tiger
at the grocery store,
buying ice cream
and toilet paper.

• • • • •

Dew drops on flat leaves . . .
I try not to groan out loud.
Glistening in the moonlight . . .
I roll my eyes. And then roll them again.
Gentle breezes spin the drops like marbles . . .
I can't help a bored cough.
Unlike marbles, the drops evaporate . . .
I look at Mrs. Little. She is loving it.
As the breeze reveals itself to be breath . . .
Wait. What?
Of a dragon, long since thought dead . . .
Dragon? Awesome!
Everyone claps.
I clap the hardest.

• • • • •

Two muffins. More Coke. Five more poets.
Mrs. Little stands,
smooths wrinkles out of her skirt.
I stand, too.
Crumbs fall from my shirt.
A man walks over to her.
They hug.
This is my youngest son.
I am confused. I'm not her son.
But then I realize,
the dragon poem poet from the stage
is her son.
Maybe a little older than Patrick.
His teeth are whitewhitewhite.
He shakes my hand.
Nice to meet you, Kevin. I've heard so much about you.
I look at Mrs. Little.
She's smiling. Her face is soft.
I think I'm smiling, too.

MONDAY

Best night.
It's all I can say
because there are too many words
to sort through.

BEATNIK'S BREWS
POETRY NIGHT

Come share your best (or worst) work at

Friday's open mic night. All ages welcome.

Poetry slammin' starts at 8.

Be there or be square!

TUESDAY

Robin does not think I am
Talented
or
Smart.
But he does think I am
Fragile
A poet
especially after he made Giant John
sit on me at recess
so he could rub my old notebook in the dirt
and then in my face.
Who's tough now?
The words, over and over, out of his mouth
like dirty flies.
Who's tough now?
Who's tough now?

Until the words turn red,
And drip on the dirt.
And there's a cut on my hand,
from a tooth
attached to a mouth
that isn't saying
Who's tough now?
anymore.

• • • • •

For a minute I think a bird is attacking,
shrieking.
But then I see it's Kelly.
The shrieking is coming from her face.
Her open mouth.
Her eyes, squinched and angry.

She flies at us, her wings wide,
and I'm afraid she's going to hit me, too.

Instead, her sneaker connects with Robin.
A soft spot
under his ribs.
There is a slow-motion *ooooof.*
And we're apart.
Until we aren't anymore.

Robin's moth face is dusty,
his teeth are pink from blood
with darker red parts
in the shadowy places
between each tooth.

And he's on me.
And it hurts.
And I hit back.
And there is more shrieking.

And I can't catch my breath.

And I scramble, kicking, because I'm on my back.

And I want to be standing.

And I feel like I'm drowning in dust and screams.

And a hand grabs my shirt collar

And a voice yells *enough!* ENOUGH!

And it's not Mrs. Smithson.

And I see her through the dust, far away.

And my arms are swinging like puppet arms.

And are made of jagged rock.

And I don't know what's happening anymore.

TIME STANDS STILL (AKA: HARTWICK'S OFFICE) ((AGAIN))

Dirt and blood on her skirt form the same shape
as the stain on the ceiling.

I stare at her skirt.
Trying to forget her hands on my shirt, my arms,
her voice shouting,
Kevin!
Kevin!
Stop it!
Enough!

My heart beating so fast.
Just think of the look on Hartwick's face
if my heart explodes
like a water balloon
smashed in a shirt pocket.

Every day I watch this nonsense from the window.
Mrs. Little is breathing fast.
Her hands clenched. Angry.
She is a dragon,
heating up the office,
growing bigger with every word.

This is not the answer, she says,
giving the hieroglyph eye to Mrs. Smithson,
who is here, too.
Having them sort it out Lord of the Flies *style?*
Not.
Working.
It.
Has.
To.
Stop.
The words are ten feet tall.
They are a fortress,
shielding only me
from the angry dragon breath.

• • • • •

Harry shakes on Mrs. Smithson's face.
Obviously, the boy can stand up for himself.
There is spit in the corners of her mouth.
She is not a dragon,
more like a donkey.
His disciplinary file proves that.

I am afraid Mrs. Little
might burst into flames.

She looks at Hartwick.
Who is contacting the superintendent, then?
Shall it be you?
Or me?
I don't know who that is, but it's a magic word
erasing color from faces
just like a bleach pen
on a blood stain.

• • • • •

Clearly, this cannot continue.
Robin looks at the floor.
I look at the stain.

Hartwick gives his speech.
You boys need a truce,
RIGHT NOW.
We clear this up,
TODAY.

I shake Robin's hand.
So small in my own.
I don't mean it.
He doesn't mean it.
Except I sort of do.
I'm sorry for what I've done.
I'm sorry I made him hate me.
I'm sorry he turned me into jagged rock.
I wonder if he is sorry, too.

• • • • •

As a sidenote,
I have composed an ode
to Hartwick's tie:

[Clearing throat noise here]

O, Principal's tie
Is this the last time we'll meet?
That makes me super happy
Because you smell like feet

• • • • •

I hear them coming up the front walk,
talking in sandpaper voices,
whacking guitar cases on the door frame
as they come inside.

My homework is on my lap
but it might as well be on Mars
as much as I have seen anything on the paper
in the past hour.

A head peeks into my room.
It's the boy who is
starting to not look like everyone else
and look like his own self
with his dark slashy hair
and his always half-open eyes.

Got any more rhymes?
I stare at him as if he is on Mars, too.
Is he joking?
Teasing me?
I reach for a crumpled page.
This is about ugly monkeys, I say.
I wrote it about you.

He looks me up and down and then laughs,
a big donkey hee-haw sound that fills up my room.

You want to come watch? he asks.

Watch what?

He rattles the paper. *The song. Are you brain-dead?*

I will be when Petey finds me in his room.
But I go with this kid anyway.
Because, yeah.
I do want to watch it.
I do want to watch them sing my song.

WEDNESDAY

Enemy status dissolved?
Superintendent is also a word for
Robin's dad.
Who knew?

• • • • •

Robin holds out my journal.
Dirty,
scratched,
torn in places.
Just like me.

I take it back.
Kelly oversees the exchange.

• • • • •

I'm sorry, you know.
My voice is crinkly. I cough.

Robin turns around
because he had already started walking away.
His lips are scrunched together.
A wadded-up-bubble-gum shape of a mouth.
He scratches at the scab over his eye.

Aren't you sorry? I ask.

He doesn't say anything.
He just walks away.

• • • • •

At lunch I sit with Kelly.
For the first time.
She has peanut butter and jelly
like a first-grader.
But I don't say anything.

She slides a piece of paper to me.
It is a poem.
It has a unicorn in it.
I give her my best hieroglyph eye.

• • • • •

I have decided something.
Freckles are not like connect the dots at all.
They are like stars. Galaxies.
They hide stories of bravery.
They hide poems about unicorns.

Unicorns that eat teachers.

THURSDAY

Today I am thirteen.
The start of a new year.
I don't feel that different
but I know I am.

• • • • •

Six presents on the table.
One from
Mom
Dad
Petey
Philip
Paul
and one with stamps mailed from Patrick.
I open them one by one.
They are all the same.
Six new notebooks.
I laugh out loud.
Mom says,
For our poet.
Dad says,
The next Hemingway.
I say,
Hemingway wasn't a poet, Dad.
Petey says,
Nerd.
I laugh again
even though Petey just kicked me under the table,
and Mom is already checking her voice mail.

• • • • •

Petey grabs me by the shirt.
Hey.
His voice is low in my ear.
You know that blue notebook? The one with the skull?
I nod.
Maybe you should use that to write songs.
You know,
for the band.
I blink a couple of times.
You mean the Shrieking Tornadoes?
He looks at me.
Really looks at me
for a long time.
That's our name, huh?
I shrug. *Those are the sounds you make.*
With your guitars.
Petey laughs. *Yeah, then. Use the notebook for that.*
For songs.
For the Shrieking Tornadoes.
I nod. *Thanks for letting me in the band.*
I almost whisper it. Can it be true?
Petey laughs again. *You're not in the band, turd.*
He taps the notebook.
Just lay down some rhymes. Okay?
Oh. Okay. Cool.
Cool.

• • • • •

Paul walks me to school
even though it makes him late.

He tells me he's proud of me.
He says he's sorry no one else ever says that.

I swat at him with one of my new notebooks.
Paul is so annoying.

(But his words were nice.
Even when he was yelling at me to quit whacking him.)

• • • • •

811.6
The real poetry section.
This red book is new,
not bent or scuffed,
no plastic cover.
The author's name is K. Jamison
just like me.
My heart speeds up, my eyes focus tight.
A hand rests on my shoulder, it's a quiet smile.

Inside the book,
my poems.
The ones I showed Mrs. Little.
Bound together.
In a real book.
Like a real poet.

FRIDAY

Shelving books, just like every day.
No detention needed.
This is my job now.
A job that needs shining eyes and soft fingers.
Jagged stones need not apply.

I take deep breaths of the library smell,
the book smell,
the soft, shiny, safe smell.

A note from Mrs. Little says:
There's another poetry night in one month.
You better get started, yes?

And the only easy prey
as far as my eyes can see
are a million words
on a million pages
just waiting.

I pull a pen from my pocket,
open up my notebook.

So many
words.
So little
time.

I have spoken!
As so often before.
But now with a smile,

"I must have somebody in a cradle," she said almost tartly, "and you are the littlest. A cradle is such a nice homely thing to have about a house."

While she sewed they played around her; such a group of happy faces and dancing limbs lit up by that romantic fire. It had become a very familiar scene, this, in the home under the ground, but we are looking on it for the last time.

There was a step above, and Wendy, you may be sure, was the first to recognize it.

"Children, I hear your father's step. He likes you to meet him at the door."

Above, the redskins crouched before Peter.

"Watch well, braves. I have spoken."

And then, as so often before, the gay children dragged him from his tree. As so often before, but never again.

He had brought nuts for the boys as well as the correct time for Wendy.

"Peter, you just spoil them, you know," Wendy simpered [exaggerated a smile]

"Ah, old lady," said Peter, hanging up his gun.

"It was me told him mothers are called old lady," Michael whispered to Curly.

"I complain of Michael," said Curly instantly.

The first twin came to Peter. "Father, we want to dance."

"Dance away, my little man," said Peter, who was in high good humour.

"But we want you to dance."

Peter was really the best dancer among them, but he pretended to be scandalised.

"Me! My old bones would rattle!"

"And mummy too."

"What," cried Wendy, "the mother of such an armful, dance!"

"But on a Saturday night," Slightly insinuated.

It was not really Saturday night, at least it may have been, for they had long lost count of the days; but always if they wanted to do anything special they said this was Saturday night, and then they did it.

Peter Pan

Acknowledgments

I'd like to thank my incomparable agent, Ammi-Joan Paquette, who gets all the credit in the world for seeing this manuscript and saying yes. (She gets extra credit for all the times she shakes her head at me and says, "Not quite, but keep trying.")

I'd also like to thank the supportive and fiercely talented group of women I spent a lovely autumn week with at a Highlights Foundation workshop in Honesdale, Pennsylvania. Extra sloppy kisses go to our faculty: Sonya Sones, Virginia Euwer Wolff, and Linda Oatman High. (And special thanks to Linda for saying, "Ooh, I like the band name parts of this manuscript, you should add more of that.")

Thank you to my critique group, Bethany Hegedus, Vanessa Lee, and Sara Kocek, for not only knowing how to give a great critique, but for knowing when it's time to just stare at the ceiling and quietly eat chocolate.

Thanks to my Spiderhouse coffee shop crew for not judging me when I eat breakfast tacos instead of writing. (And a high five to E. Kristin Anderson, who mentioned found poetry and how she thought it would improve the first draft.)

To everyone in the Austin, Texas, SCBWI, you guys are the epitome of awesome. (And a shout-out to Nikki Loftin, Donna Bowman Bratton, and Liz Garton Scanlon for reading early drafts and assuring me I wasn't insane to want these words to be a book.)

Even though they hate my comfy writing pants, I will still thank my kiddos, Sam, Georgia, and Isaac, for dealing with the whims of a crazy mom writing a book. And an extra million billion thanks go to my husband, Steven, for knowing that sometimes I have to run away and write write write.

Last but most definitely not least, huge, huge thanks to everyone at Chronicle, especially Tamra Tuller, who has laughed and agonized and sniffled over Kevin just as much as I have.

O, PRINCIPAL'S TIE,

NECKTIE POEMS

O, Principal's tie
You are so fly
Like someone poking me
IN MY EYE

FLEA BAT?

Fleas!

• • • • •

O, Principal's tie
You should run free
That way maybe you can escape
All of your fleas

• • • • •

tie

O, Principal's tie
You remind me of that time
I saw a TV show
About fashion crime

Ugly →

YUCK →

you are so gross, like six-day-old peanut butter toast.

. . . . .

O, Principal's tie
You make me want to growl
Because you smell
SO FOWL. FOUL.

. . . . . .

O, Principal's tie
You give me ten million creeps
Because you smell like
Ten million sheeps.

TERRIBLE!